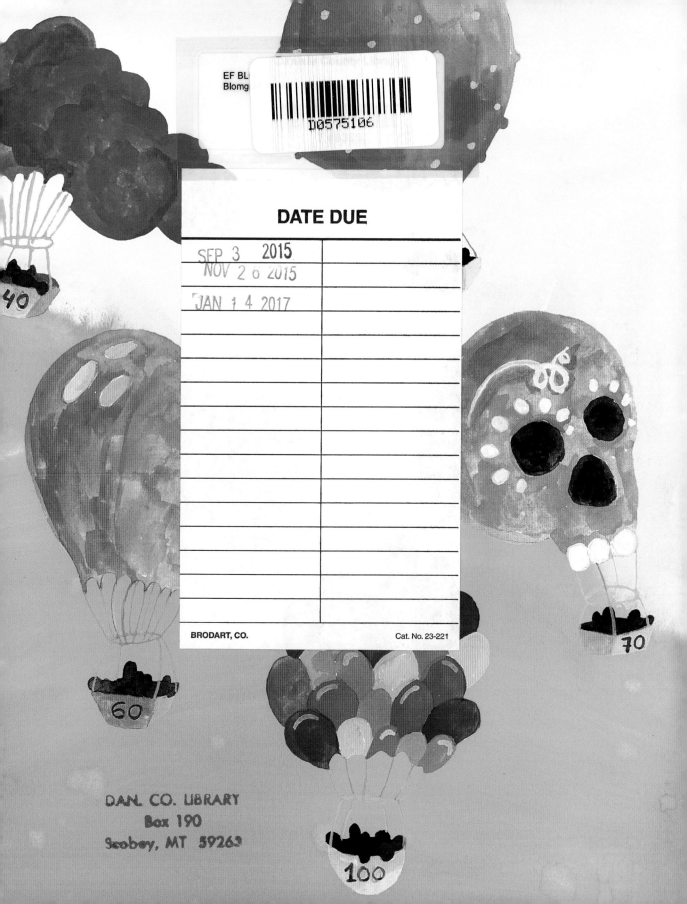

First American Edition 2015
Kane Miller, A Division of EDC Publishing

Text and illustrations © 2014 Lidia Blomgren
First published in 2014 by Alfabeta Bokförlag AB with the Swedish title *Tio Gorillor*

For information contact:
Kane Miller, A Division of EDC Publishing
PO Box 470663
Tulsa, OK 74147-0663
www.kanemiller.com
www.edcpub.com
www.usbornebooksandmore.com

Library of Congress Control Number: 2014949834

Printed in Latvia

1 2 3 4 5 6 7 8 9 10

ISBN: 978-1-61067-380-8

Ten Gorillas

Lidia Blomgren

Kane Miller
A DIVISION OF EDC PUBLISHING

Ten gorillas
wearing glasses.

Twenty chimpanzees pulling the cat's tail. Naughty chimps!

20

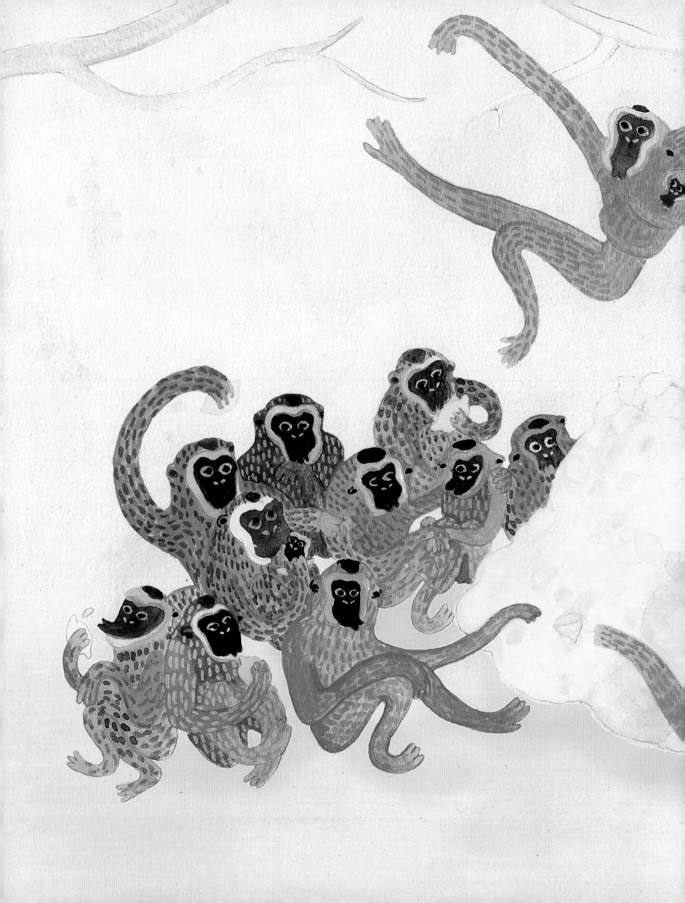

30

Thirty gibbons ...
and not a single cell phone
between them.

Forty tamarins
waiting patiently – well,
most of them – for cupcakes.

One of these mandrills
doesn't like candy ...

... but the forty-nine others do.

$$49 + 1 = 50$$

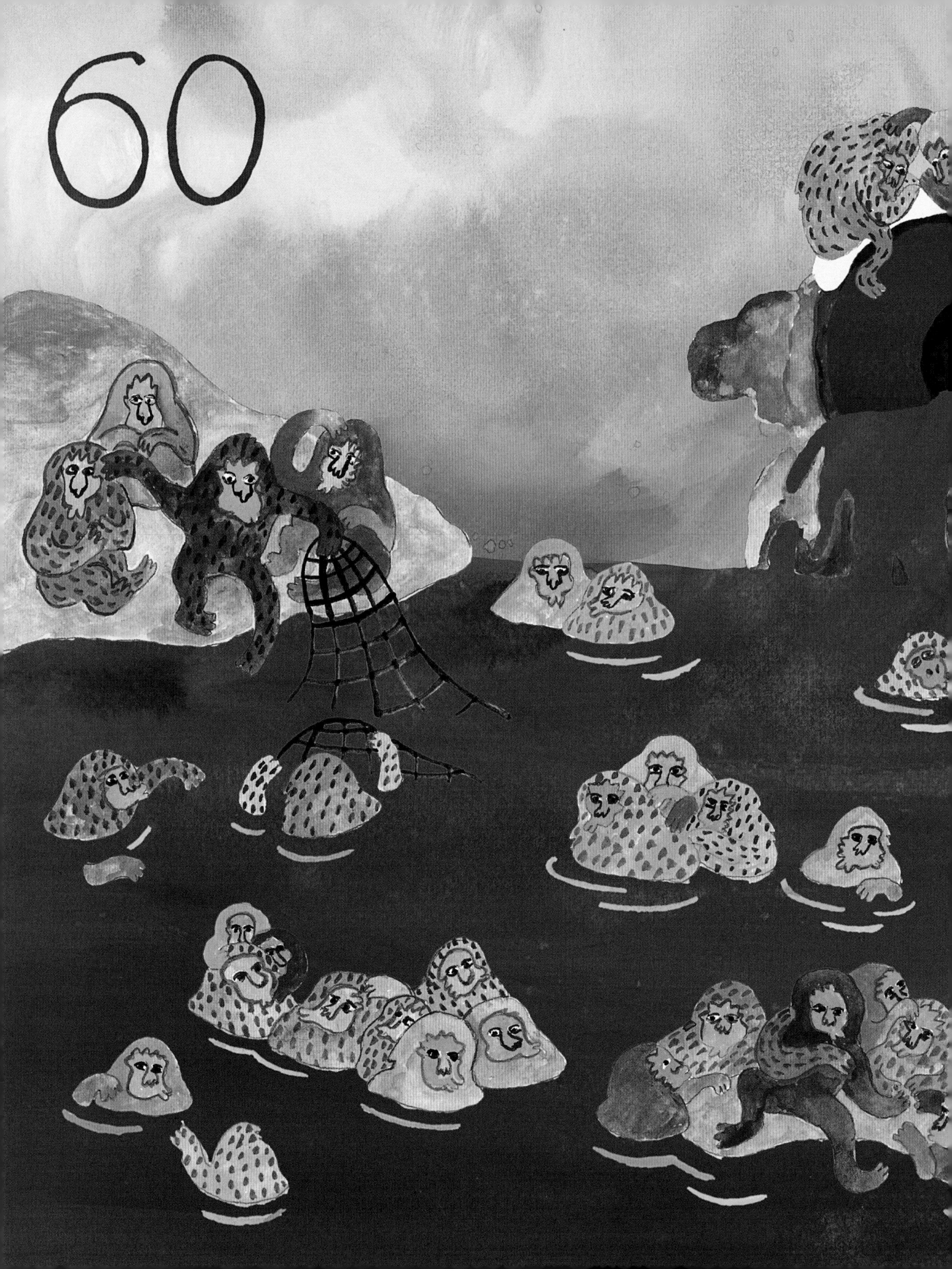
60

Sixty macaques
fishing in the sewer! Yuck!

Seventy baboons
picking bananas.

Eighty-two guenons
hanging out in hammocks.

Ninety spider monkeys climbing skyscrapers. What a racket!

One hundred
orangutans frolicking
in the fjords.

552

A troop of apes!
A tribe of monkeys!
How many in all?
Too many to fit in just
one hot air balloon!